The story of Noah's Ark
As seen through the eyes of an imaginative boy

Alex's Wonder ARK Adventure

Written By
Sally Jane

Edited by
Andrew Thompson

WestBow Press books may be ordered through booksellers or by contacting:

WestBow Press
A Division of Thomas Nelson & Zondervan
1663 Liberty Drive
Bloomington, IN 47403
www.westbowpress.com
1 (866) 928-1240

ISBN: 978-1-4908-6980-3 (sc)
ISBN: 978-1-4908-6979-7 (e)

Library of Congress Control Number: 2015902327

Print information available on the last page.

WestBow Press rev. date: 02/18/2015

WestBow®
PRESS
A DIVISION OF THOMAS NELSON
& ZONDERVAN

This children's story is dedicated to my four children and three grandchildren. To my oldest son Matthew who was my first adventurous boy. To my daughter Karen who helped in the completion of this book. To my son Andrew who helped with editing. To my youngest son Alex who has always loved Sunday school and Bible stories, and is the inspiration for this adventure! Finally, to my three beautiful grandchildren: Jacob, Joshua, and Elizabeth who I love very much.

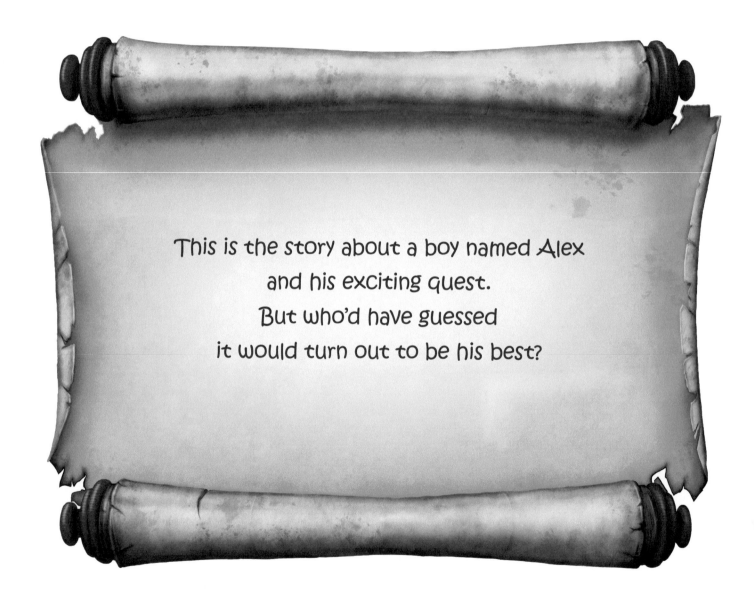

This is the story about a boy named Alex
and his exciting quest.
But who'd have guessed
it would turn out to be his best?

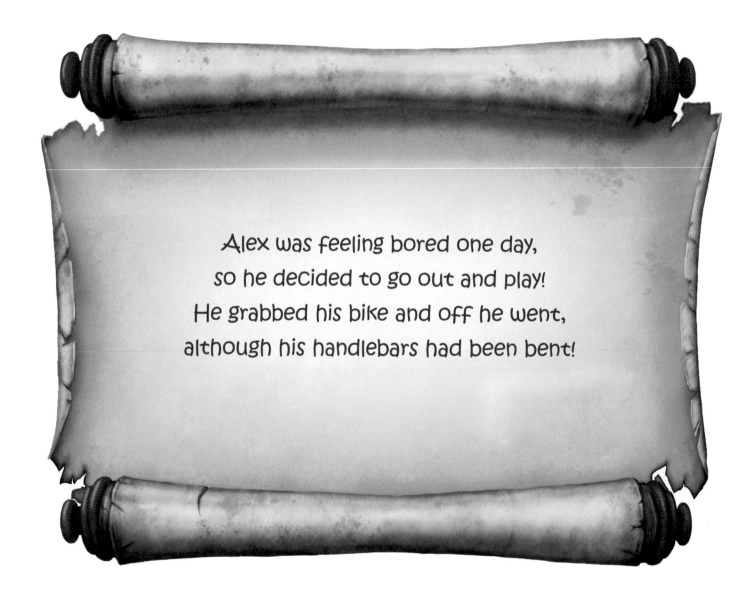

Alex was feeling bored one day,
so he decided to go out and play!
He grabbed his bike and off he went,
although his handlebars had been bent!

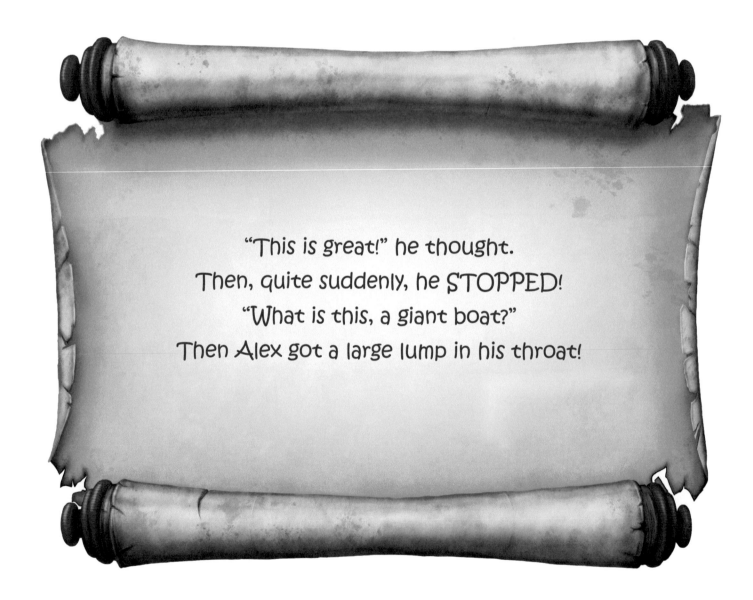

"This is great!" he thought.
Then, quite suddenly, he STOPPED!
"What is this, a giant boat?"
Then Alex got a large lump in his throat!

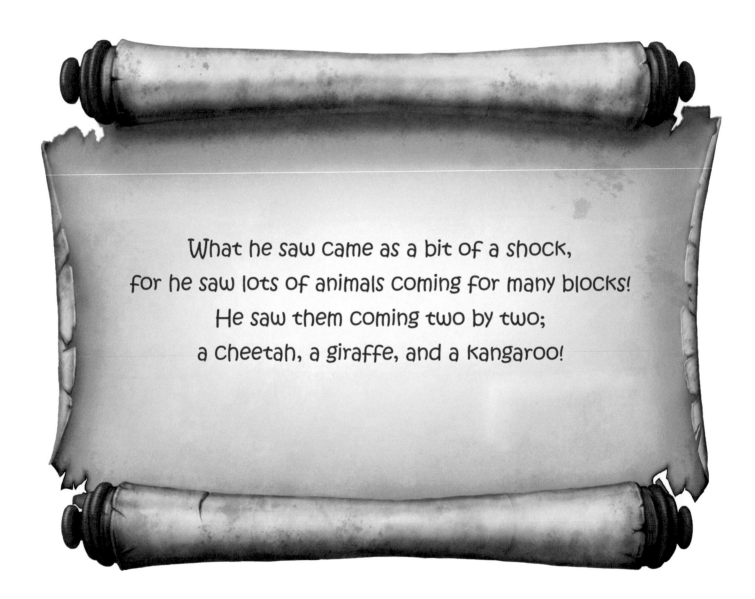

What he saw came as a bit of a shock,
for he saw lots of animals coming for many blocks!
He saw them coming two by two;
a cheetah, a giraffe, and a kangaroo!

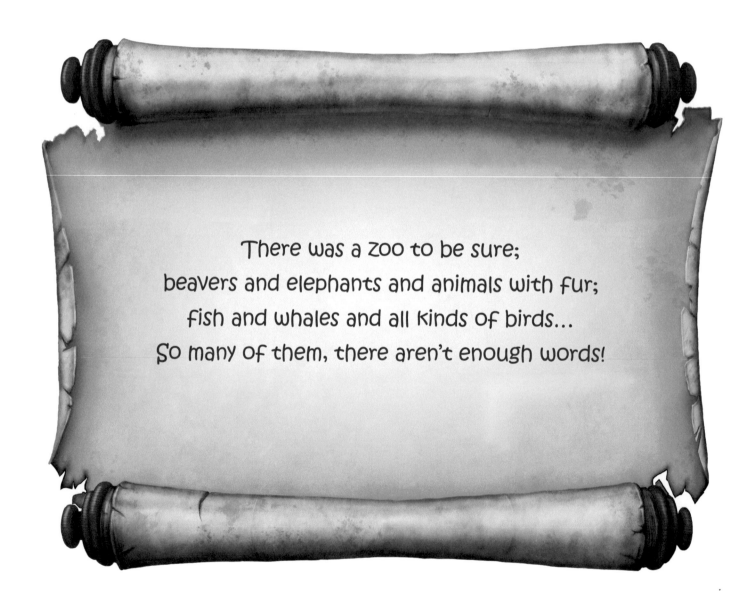

There was a zoo to be sure;
beavers and elephants and animals with fur;
fish and whales and all kinds of birds...
So many of them, there aren't enough words!

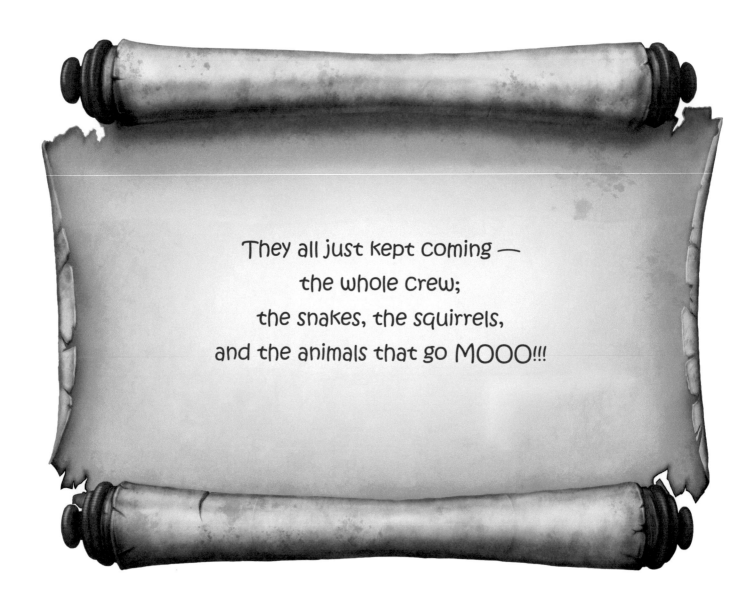

They all just kept coming —
the whole crew;
the snakes, the squirrels,
and the animals that go MOOO!!!

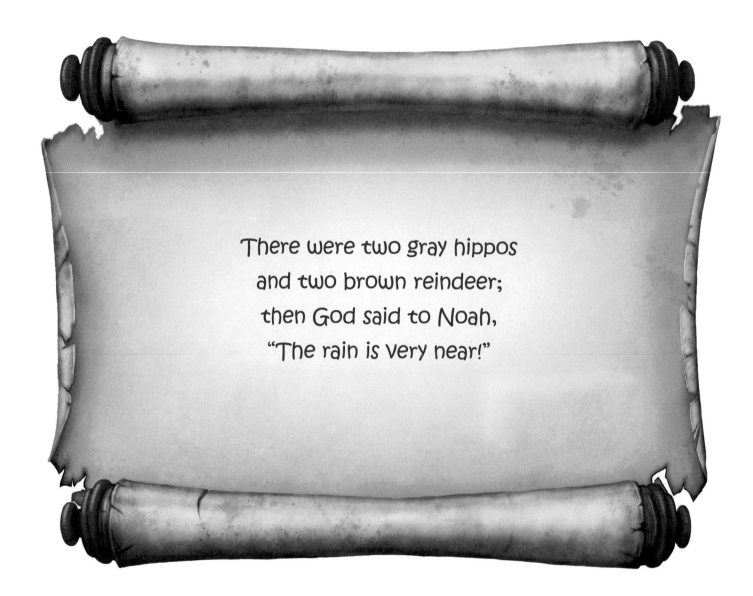

There were two gray hippos
and two brown reindeer;
then God said to Noah,
"The rain is very near!"

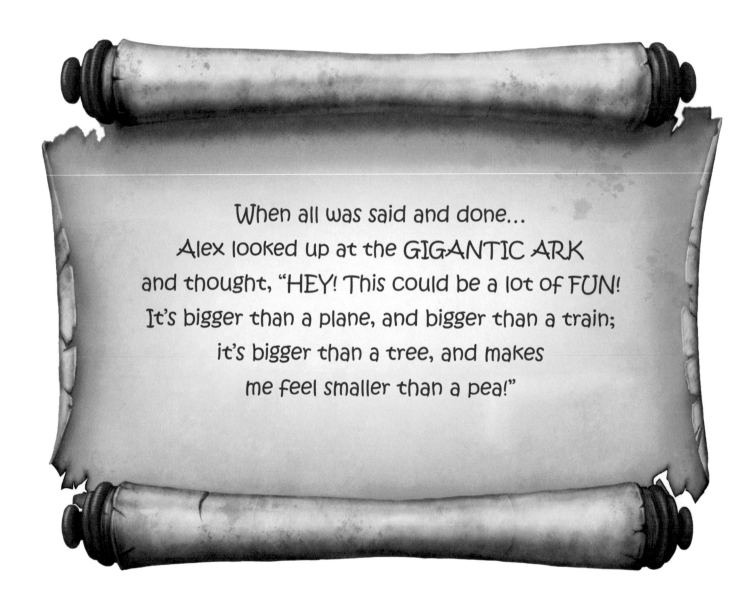

When all was said and done...
Alex looked up at the GIGANTIC ARK
and thought, "HEY! This could be a lot of FUN!
It's bigger than a plane, and bigger than a train;
it's bigger than a tree, and makes
me feel smaller than a pea!"

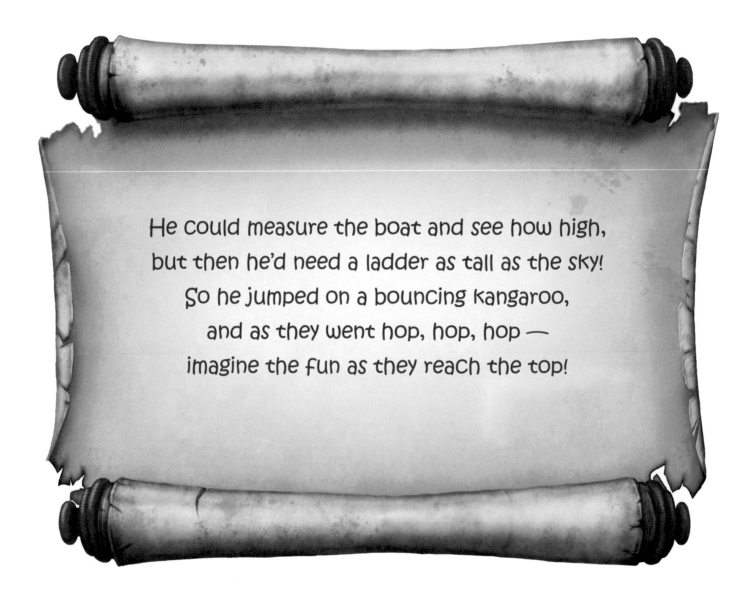

He could measure the boat and see how high,
but then he'd need a ladder as tall as the sky!
So he jumped on a bouncing kangaroo,
and as they went hop, hop, hop —
imagine the fun as they reach the top!

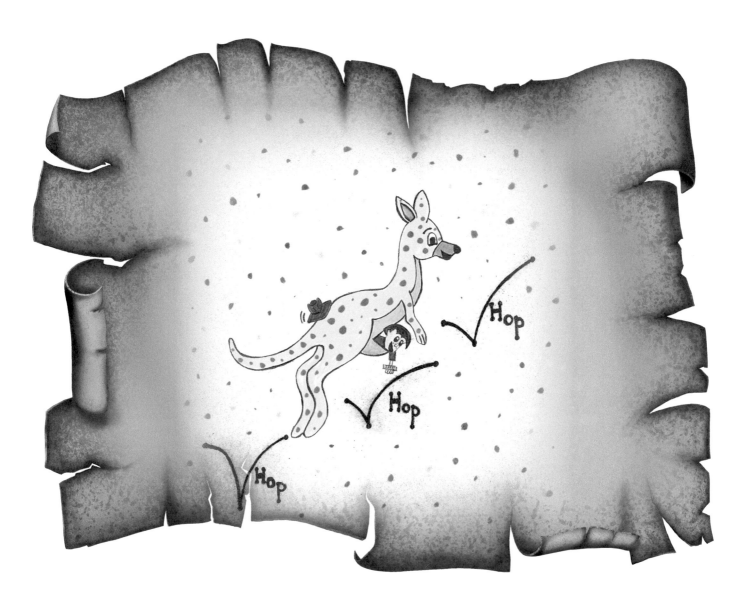

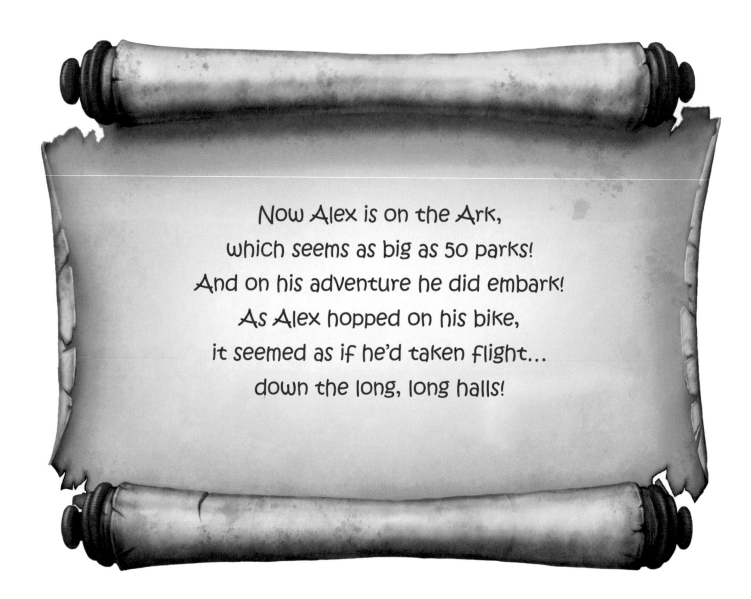

Now Alex is on the Ark,
which seems as big as 50 parks!
And on his adventure he did embark!
As Alex hopped on his bike,
it seemed as if he'd taken flight...
down the long, long halls!

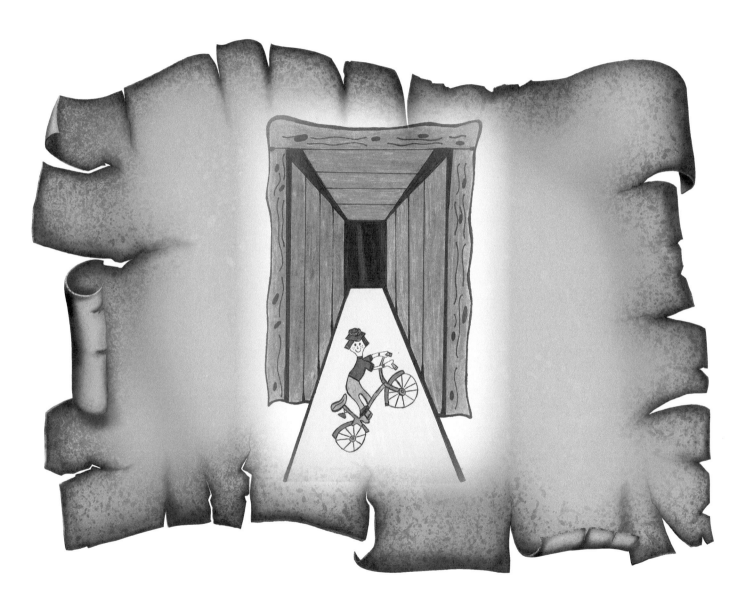

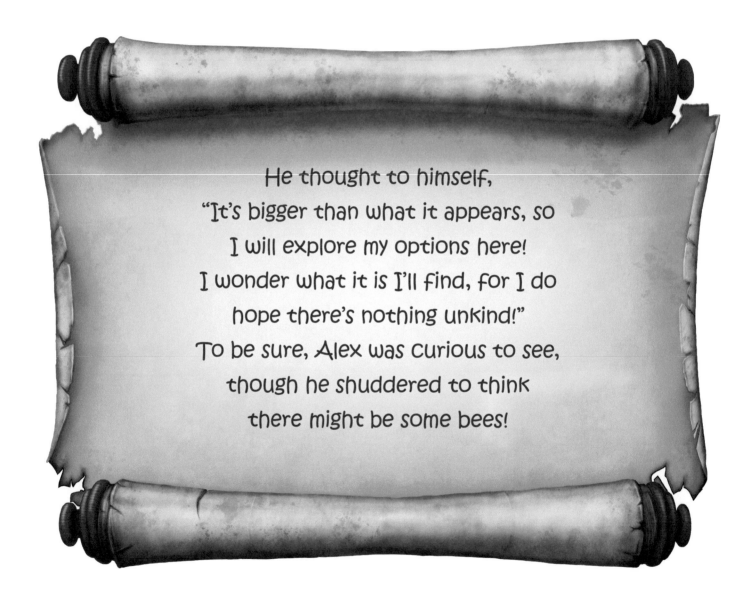

He thought to himself,
"It's bigger than what it appears, so
I will explore my options here!
I wonder what it is I'll find, for I do
hope there's nothing unkind!"
To be sure, Alex was curious to see,
though he shuddered to think
there might be some bees!

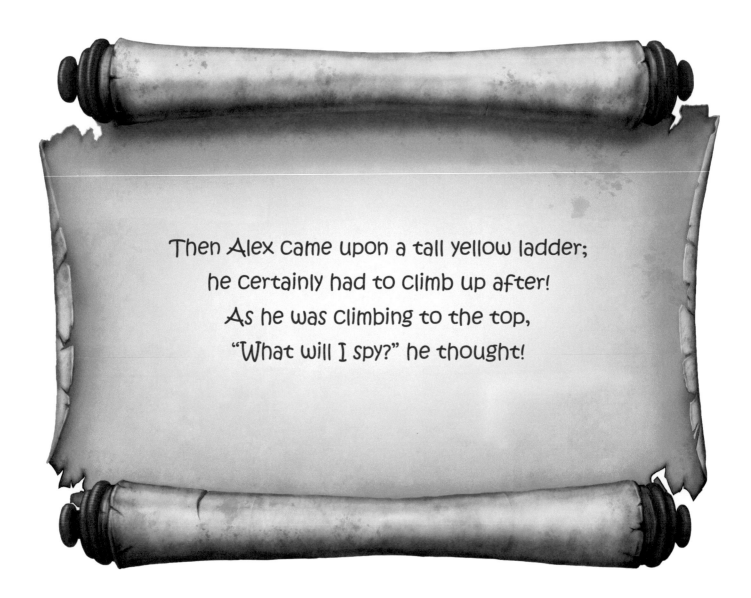

Then Alex came upon a tall yellow ladder;
he certainly had to climb up after!
As he was climbing to the top,
"What will I spy?" he thought!

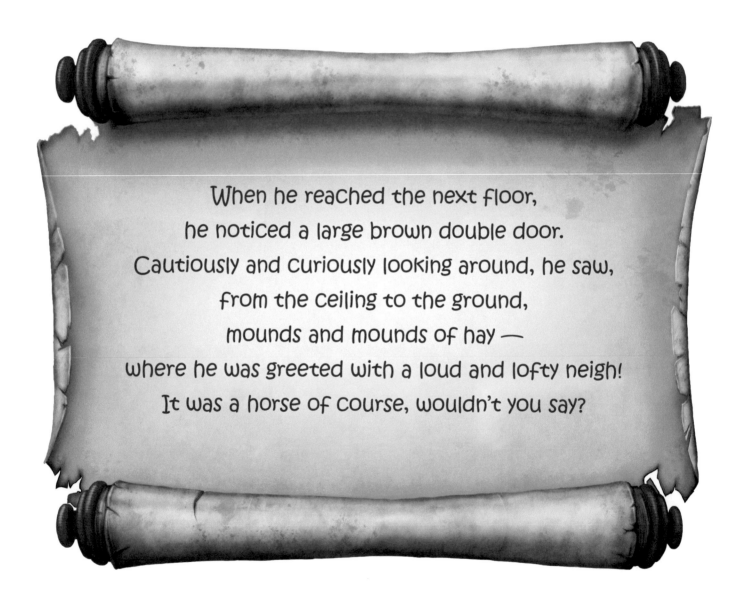

When he reached the next floor,
he noticed a large brown double door.
Cautiously and curiously looking around, he saw,
from the ceiling to the ground,
mounds and mounds of hay —
where he was greeted with a loud and lofty neigh!
It was a horse of course, wouldn't you say?

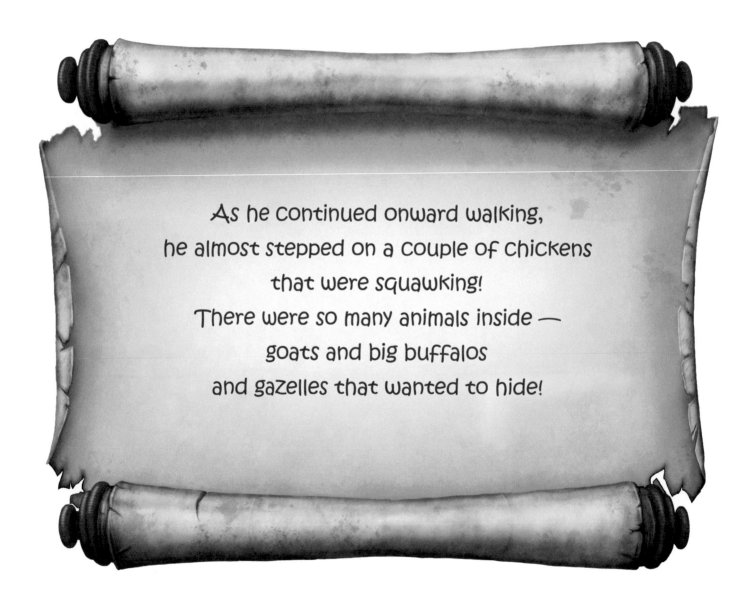

As he continued onward walking,
he almost stepped on a couple of chickens
that were squawking!
There were so many animals inside —
goats and big buffalos
and gazelles that wanted to hide!

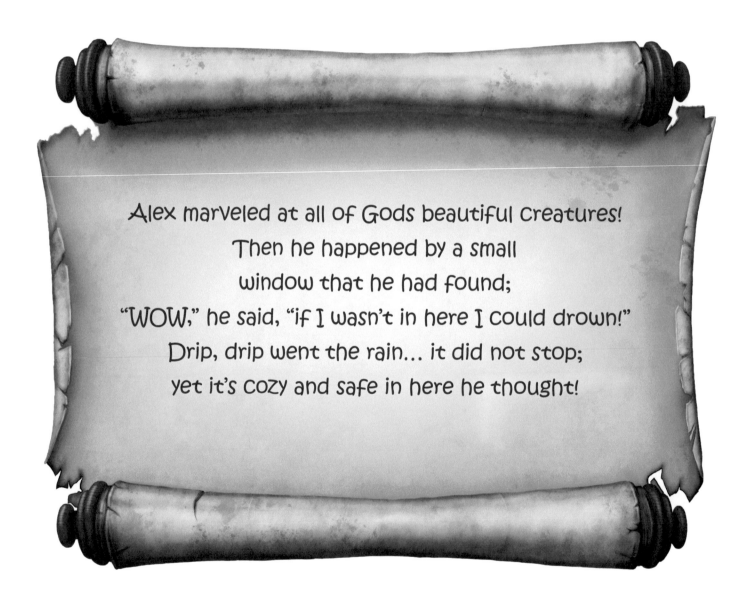

Alex marveled at all of Gods beautiful creatures!
Then he happened by a small
window that he had found;
"WOW," he said, "if I wasn't in here I could drown!"
Drip, drip went the rain… it did not stop;
yet it's cozy and safe in here he thought!

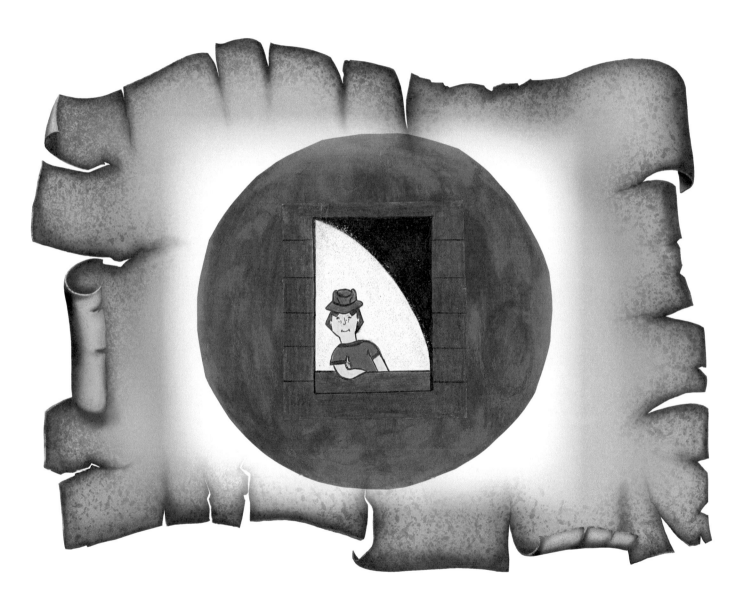

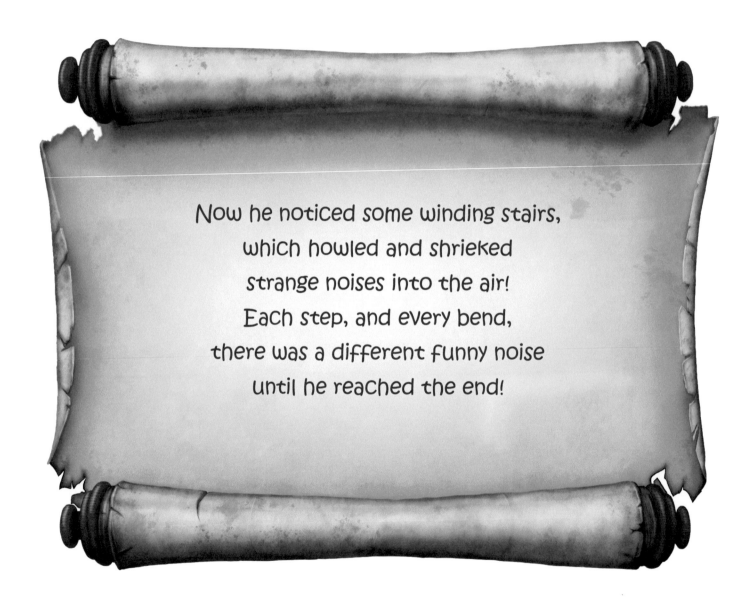

Now he noticed some winding stairs,
which howled and shrieked
strange noises into the air!
Each step, and every bend,
there was a different funny noise
until he reached the end!

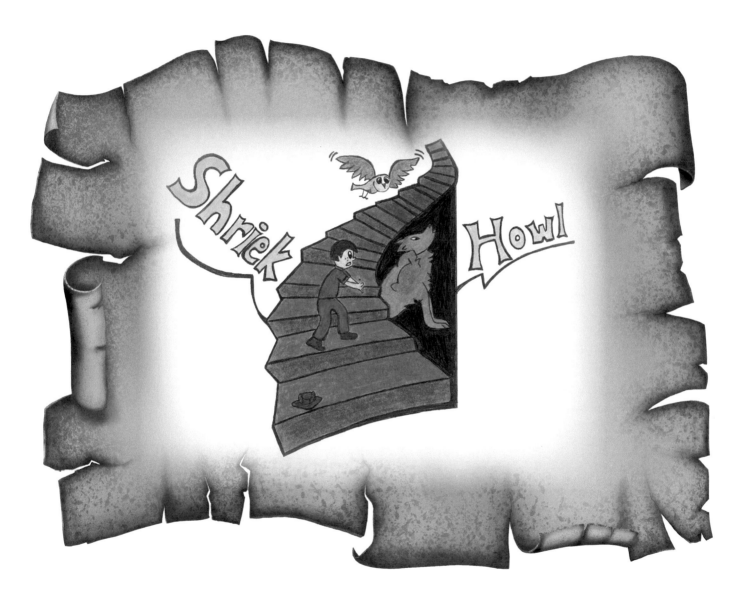

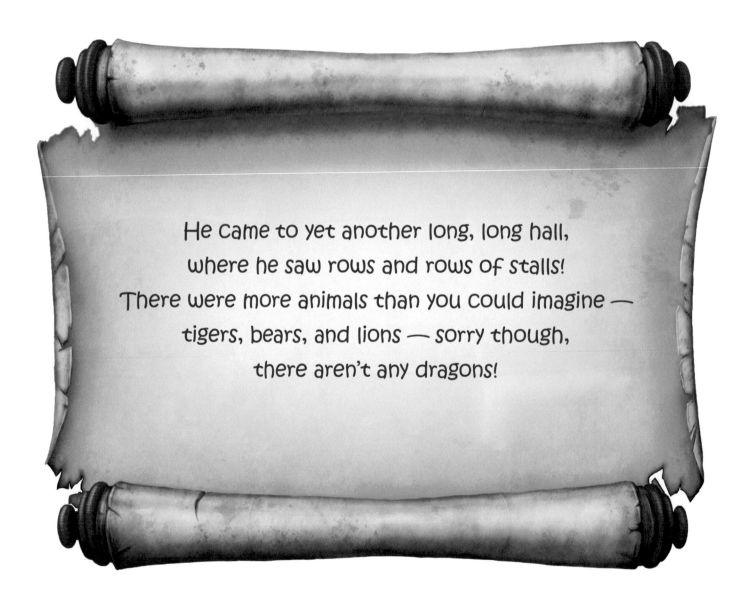

He came to yet another long, long hall,
where he saw rows and rows of stalls!
There were more animals than you could imagine —
tigers, bears, and lions — sorry though,
there aren't any dragons!

Alex started to pet the animals
and gave them lots of treats!
Wishing he could have just one
to take home and keep!

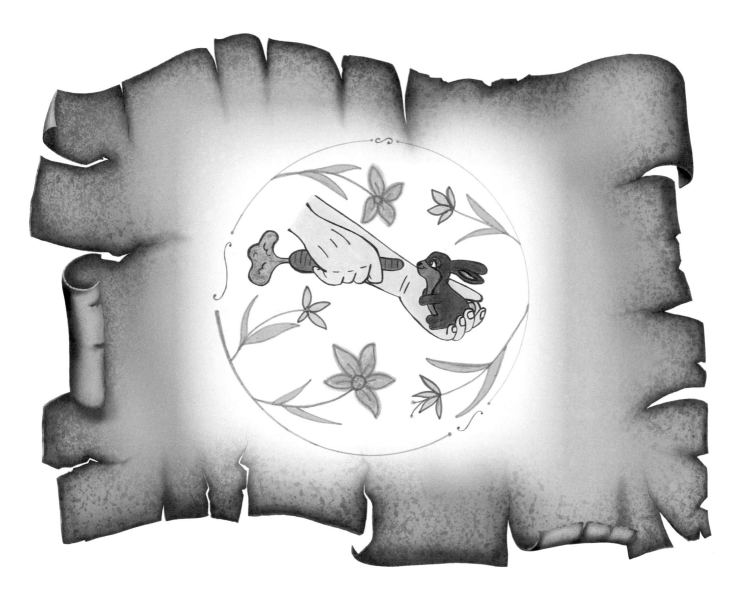

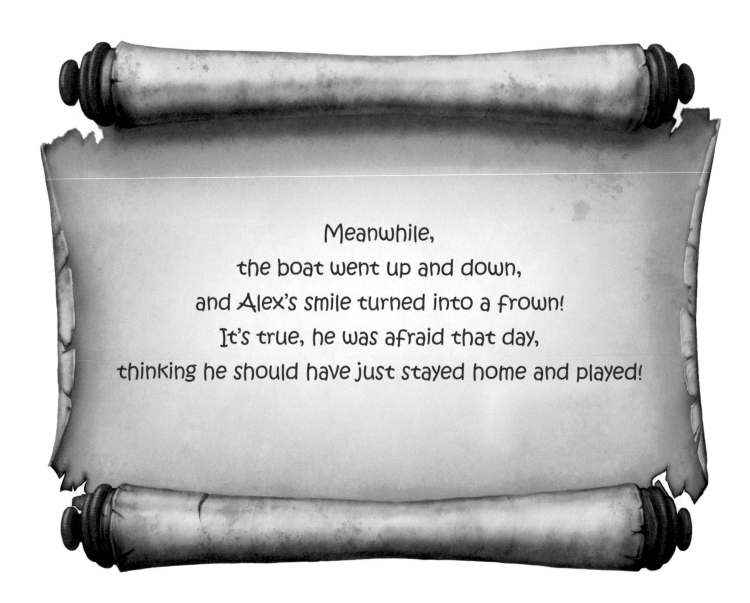

Meanwhile,
the boat went up and down,
and Alex's smile turned into a frown!
It's true, he was afraid that day,
thinking he should have just stayed home and played!

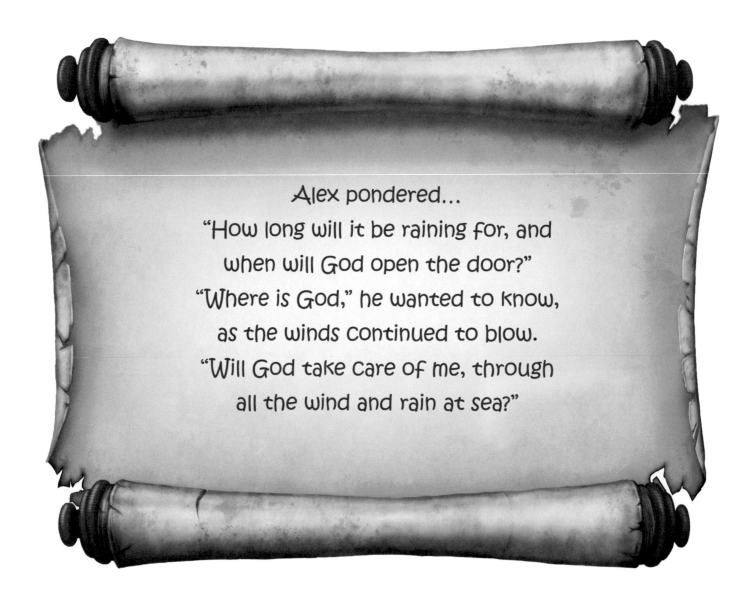

Alex pondered...

"How long will it be raining for, and
when will God open the door?"
"Where is God," he wanted to know,
as the winds continued to blow.
"Will God take care of me, through
all the wind and rain at sea?"

But quite unexpectedly the rain did stop!
He couldn't even hear one small PLOP!!

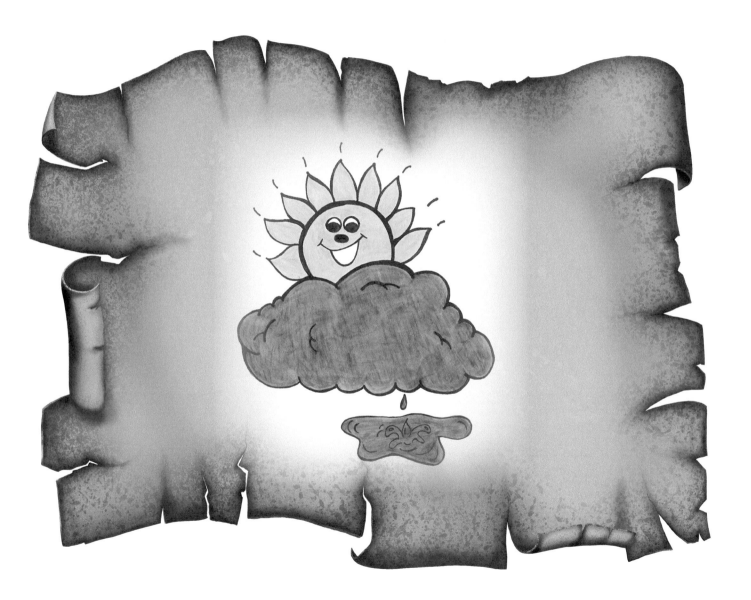

Then softly he heard a voice so near...
It was God speaking in his left ear!

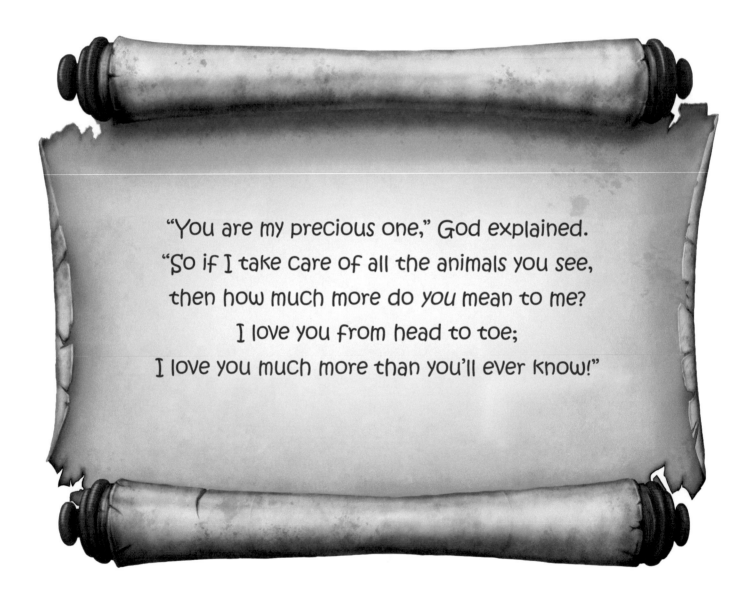

"You are my precious one," God explained.
"So if I take care of all the animals you see,
then how much more do *you* mean to me?
I love you from head to toe;
I love you much more than you'll ever know!"

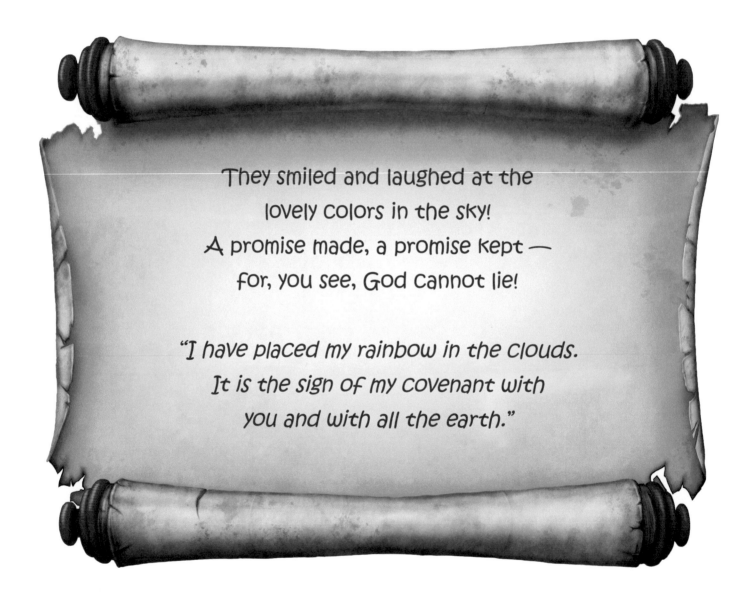

They smiled and laughed at the
lovely colors in the sky!
A promise made, a promise kept —
for, you see, God cannot lie!

"I have placed my rainbow in the clouds.
It is the sign of my covenant with
you and with all the earth."

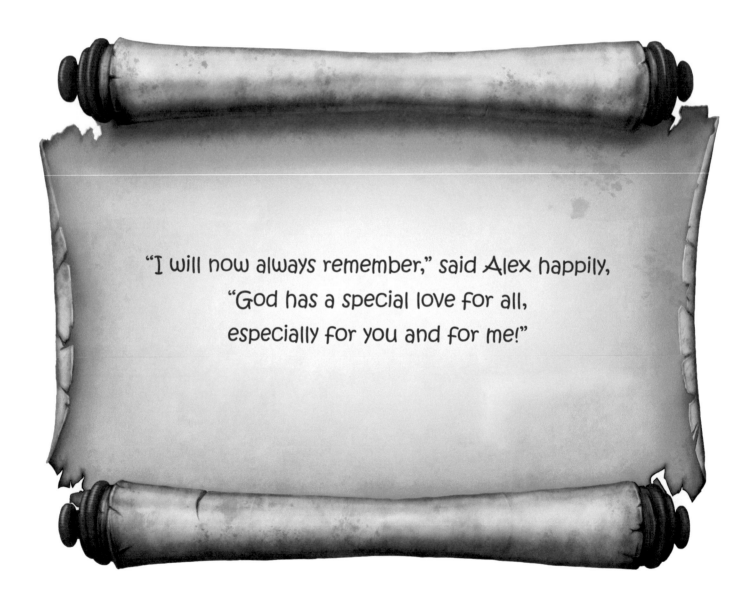

"I will now always remember," said Alex happily,
"God has a special love for all,
especially for you and for me!"

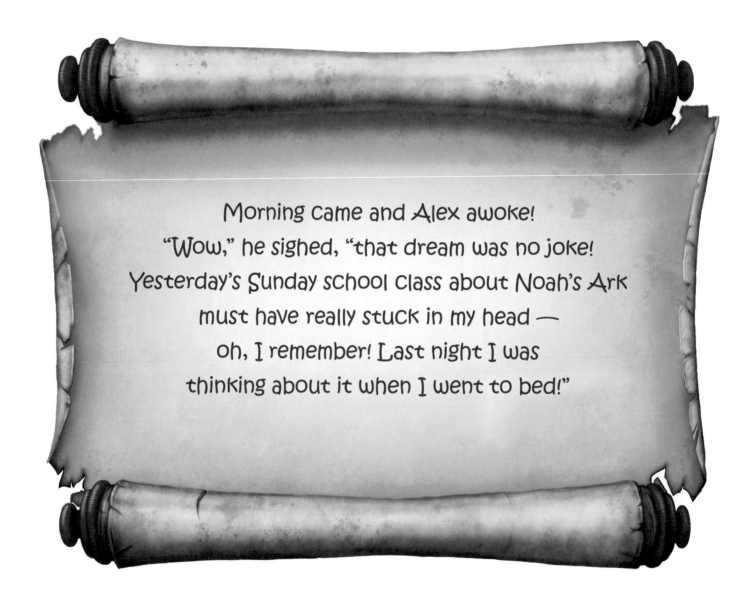

Morning came and Alex awoke!
"Wow," he sighed, "that dream was no joke!
Yesterday's Sunday school class about Noah's Ark
must have really stuck in my head —
oh, I remember! Last night I was
thinking about it when I went to bed!"

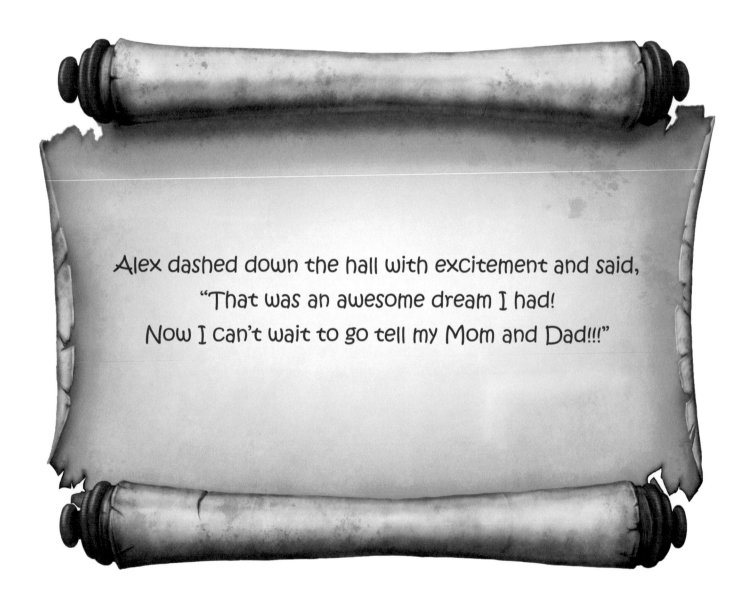

Alex dashed down the hall with excitement and said,
"That was an awesome dream I had!
Now I can't wait to go tell my Mom and Dad!!!"

Printed in the United States
By Bookmasters